TRAPPED

Rigby is an imprint of Pearson Education Limited, a company incorporated in England and Wales, having its registered office at Edinburgh Gate, Harlow, Essex, CM20 2JE.
Registered company number: 872828
www.rigbyed.co.uk

Rigby is a registered trademark of Reed Elsevier Inc, Licensed to Pearson Education Limited

Trapped first published 2002

Series editor: Wendy Wren

12
13

Trapped   ISBN 978 0 433078 53 1
Group Reading Pack with Teaching Notes   ISBN 978 0 433078 59 3

Illustrated by David Barnett, Tony Morris, Chris Pepper
Cover illustration © Max Ellis 2002
Repro by Digital Imaging, Glasgow
Printed in China (CTPS/13)

THE CORAL ISLAND

by R M Ballantyne
Adapted by Tony Bradman

 **ONE**

My name is Ralph, and I have a great passion for roaming the wide world. That's hardly surprising – I come from a long line of seafarers, on both sides of my family. I was even born at sea. My father made his living as a ship's captain, and my mother went with him on many a long voyage.

By all accounts it was a wild, black night of howling storms on the Atlantic Ocean, the night that I was born. My parents often told me the story, and many other terrifying tales of tempests and shipwrecks, and I suppose that should have put me off the idea of becoming a sailor myself. But alas, none of it did. In fact, the more salty yarns I heard, the more I wanted to go to sea.

We lived in a small fishing village on the coast, and whenever my father was at home I pestered him to take me to the harbour to look at the boats and talk to the sailors and fishermen. And eventually, when I was twelve or so, I persuaded him to let me become an apprentice on a coasting vessel.

For the next few years, I sailed up and down the coast, learning my trade as a sailor. I got on well with my shipmates, and met many sailors who had travelled to almost every part of the world. I loved hearing their tales of wild adventures and terrible storms, of the dangers they had survived, and the strange and exotic places and animals and people they had encountered.

But what fascinated me most were their stories of the southern seas, and of the coral islands of the Pacific. I longed to see these beautiful islands in the tropical sun, with their lush vegetation and white beaches, their reefs formed by tiny creatures. By the time I was fifteen, I was determined to go.

At first, my parents said they didn't want me to travel that far away, but I managed to convince them it was the right thing for me to do. So my father spoke to an old friend of his, the captain of a merchant ship, a large vessel called *The Arrow*, which would soon be bound for the Pacific Ocean.

A few days later I went on board, and we set sail that same morning.

I was very excited as I stood on the deck waving to my parents, the breeze filling the canvas sails above my head, the salt tang of the sea in my nostrils.

Little did I know then what an amazing adventure lay in store for me.

TWO

There were several boys on the ship, and I made friends with two of them.

Jack was eighteen, a tall, broad-shouldered lad. He was mild and quiet, but clever, and good-humoured, too. We took to each other straight away. Peter was fourteen, and quite different – he was little and quick and funny, quite mischievous really, although his mischief was completely harmless.

And me? I was hard-working, and serious most of the time. But I was also inquisitive, and I liked to laugh. So I suppose you could say Jack and Peter and I made a good team – which is just as well, considering what happened.

It was a fine ship and crew, and the voyage went smoothly as we sailed south through the Atlantic. We rounded Cape Horn, then headed north into the Pacific, and soon we were among the coral islands. I'll never forget the joy I felt as we passed the first of those pure white, dazzling shores in the sunshine. I could hardly believe that I was really there, seeing them …

One night, a terrible storm suddenly burst upon us. The howling wind carried off two of our masts, and we were driven over the sea, enormous waves crashing on the decks and sweeping away anything that wasn't lashed down. It was terrifying, but at last, as the sun rose, we saw land. It was a coral island, the waves pounding on the reef surrounding it.

"Quick, lads," the captain yelled. "Into the boat before we hit the rocks!"

Soon the ship's small lifeboat was ready to be launched, and most of the crew waiting to clamber into it. Jack, however, held Peter and me back.

"That boat will never reach the shore," he said, shouting to make himself heard above the wind, "especially if it's too crowded. I've got a much better idea."

Jack headed for the bow of the ship. Peter and I looked at each other, then we followed him, trusting our friend's judgement. Jack stopped at last, and pointed at a large oar stored by the gunwale. "Let's get this over the side," he yelled. "All we need do is cling on to it till we reach the island … "

Just then, a colossal wave hit the deck with a crash like thunder, and down came the remaining mast. It went into the water, dragging the lifeboat and crew with it.

Our oar became entangled with the rigging, and Jack seized an axe to cut it free. But he missed the rope, and the axe stuck deep in the oar.

Suddenly, another wave fell upon us, washing the oar free. Then the ship smashed into the rocks and heeled over. We staggered. I was stricken with panic, and felt certain that I was going to die. But Jack wasn't beaten yet.

"Ralph, Peter, grab the oar!" he yelled, as water foamed around our legs.

Peter and I didn't have to be told twice. We dived for the oar, and so did Jack, and I felt yet another huge wave sweeping us towards the wild sea. I saw the lifeboat whirling in the surf and the crew bobbing in the water. Then my head slammed into something, and we plunged into the water ourselves.

I held onto the oar, but darkness filled my mind, and I knew no more.

THREE

It only seemed like a few seconds later when I opened my eyes. The first thing I saw was Peter looking down at me, his face filled with anxiety.

"Speak to us, Ralph," he said. "Are you feeling better now?"

"I … I think so," I murmured.

I realised I was lying on dry land, and I sat up. Jack was beside me. I looked round and saw that we were on a beach. My head throbbed, and I discovered I had a nasty cut on my forehead, which was still bleeding.

"What happened?" I asked.

"You nearly choked me to death, that's what!" laughed Peter.

"I don't understand," I said. "I remember the oar, the waves … "

"You banged your head on something as we went over the side," Jack said, smiling at me, "which seemed to stun you. Then you grabbed Peter round the neck without realising what you were doing, and held on to him pretty tight."

"We only made it to shore thanks to good old Jack," said Peter. "I don't know how, but he got us through a gap in the reef and swam us in."

"But what of the captain and crew?" I asked. "Were they all drowned?"

"I think not," said Jack. "I saw most of the men scrambling into the lifeboat before the storm swept it away from the reef. With any luck, it will take them to one of the other islands we passed. The ship's sunk, though."

"So we're marooned," said Peter. "All alone on a desert island."

"But we might not be alone," I murmured. My head was throbbing less now, and the bleeding had stopped. I decided to try and look on the bright side. "The island might have some inhabitants, people who could help us."

"Well, I don't see much evidence of any inhabitants," said Peter.

He gestured at the beach around us, and I had to admit he was right. It stretched away as far as I could see in either direction, its perfect white sands empty of human life. Behind us was a line of palm trees, edging what looked like thick jungle. In front of the trees was a calm lagoon, little waves lapping at the shore, while bigger waves still crashed on the reef beyond.

But the storm was moving away, the sun shining in the clear blue sky.

"Besides, if there *are* any people here, they might not take kindly to us arriving on their island," whispered Peter. "They might even be cannibals!"

We stood silently for a second, letting that unpleasant thought sink in.

"Well, there's no point worrying about it," said Jack at last. "We've got to be practical. If the captain does make it to another island, he's bound to send someone to look for us. We just have to survive until they come. So we'll need to find fresh water to drink and something to eat, and build a shelter."

Jack was right, of course, and I could tell Peter felt relieved that our friend was taking charge. I did too. We were in a sticky situation, but at least the three of us could face it together. Being alone would have been far worse …

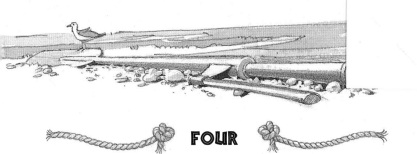

FOUR

Jack decided our first task was to take stock of what we had brought with us from the wreck. The hot sun had already dried our clothes: each of us wore our usual ship-board outfits – cotton trousers and shirts – but we'd lost our shoes in the wild sea. We sat on a large rock and emptied our pockets.

"We don't have much, do we?" said Peter, as we stared glumly at the few objects on the rock. There was a penknife with its rusty blade broken off half-way, an old pencil case, some strong cord, a sail-maker's needle, and a little ship's telescope, with the glass at the small end broken into pieces.

"The oar!" said Jack suddenly. "We've forgotten the oar!" He dashed off along the beach, Peter and I following him. "Here it is," said Jack, splashing into the shallows. We splashed in too, to help haul the oar onto the beach.

"Well, boys – this is first rate!" said Peter. As we'd pulled in the oar, it had slowly turned, revealing the axe. It had stayed stuck in the wood.

"Capital!" Jack said happily. "That's just what we need. And look, there's a piece of iron on the end of the oar – that might come in handy too."

We pulled the axe free, then took both axe and oar back to our rock. The sun was now directly overhead, and we were beginning to feel the heat.

"I say, you two," I croaked. "I would give a great deal for a drink … "

"There must be fresh water on the island somewhere," said Jack. "There's probably a spring, although it could take some time to find it. Hang on, those trees over there … I think we may be in luck! Come on, let's have a look!"

Jack led us to the jungle behind the beach, and we saw that the trees had tall, bare trunks, with clusters of round, green objects tucked under a crown of long, thick leaves at the top.

"Do you think you could climb up and get one of those, Peter?" Jack said.

Peter didn't answer. He just grinned, gripped the trunk with his hands and feet like a monkey, scrambled skywards, then returned with an unripe green coconut.

"Here you are," he said, handing it to Jack. "I can't see what good it will do us, though … And how did you know it was a coconut tree, anyway?"

"Oh, I've read a few books about the South Seas," said Jack, opening his penknife. "Books can be very useful."

Strange as it may seem these days, at that time few people in England had seen any coconuts, or even knew that such exotic fruits existed. Peter and I certainly had no idea what that smooth, green shape might contain.

Jack dug the penknife into it, made a small hole, then offered the coconut to Peter. "Clap it to your mouth, old fellow," said Jack, and smiled.

Peter did what he was told… and Jack and I both burst into laughter when we saw the change on Peter's face. His eyes grew wide with astonishment.

"It's pure nectar!" he said at last, and when I took my turn at swigging from the coconut, I had to agree with him. For it contained a sweet, cool, milky fluid rather like lemonade. And according to Jack – or at least, the books he'd read – this liquid would satisfy our hunger as well as our thirst.

We collected as many coconuts as we could carry, then spent the rest of the day building a shelter by our rock. We used the axe to cut long branches from some other trees behind the beach, and made a frame. Then we covered the frame with large palm leaves, and before long, we had a cosy little house.

Jack surprised us once more. We had no matches, but he made a fire – he wrapped some cord round a sharpened stick, placed its end on a piece of tinder wood, then spun the stick until the tinder began to grow warm and smoke. Jack added dry twigs and leaves, and soon we had a roaring fire.

As the sun set over the lagoon we sat outside our shelter, feasting on coconuts, the smoke and sparks from our fire rising into the starry sky. It had been a strange and frightening day, but there had been wonder in it as well. I had seen and done some amazing things, and I was on a coral island …

That night, the distant booming of the surf on the reef was my lullaby.

FIVE

We spent the next few days exploring the surroundings of our new home, getting used to being on the island, even enjoying ourselves a little.

Further down the beach we came across a little freshwater stream that flowed out of the jungle and into the sea – so that took care of our drinking needs. But we didn't penetrate far into the jungle itself. It seemed dark and forbidding, even in broad daylight, and we preferred the bright, open beach.

Jack and I, however, did go swimming – or rather diving – in the lagoon. And what an incredible experience that was! The water within the reef was calm, as warm as a bath, and clear from the surface to the bottom. And the reef was filled with beautiful coral formations of every size and shape.

"Look, Peter," I said one day when Jack and I surfaced from one of our dives. "We've collected lots of oysters to go with our coconuts tonight!"

"Good!" said Peter, examining our finds. "I'm beginning to grow tired of living just on coconuts. Did you see any fish down there, by the way?"

"We did, and I tried to catch one," Jack replied, "but it was impossible."

"Well, maybe I could do a little better ... " Peter said thoughtfully. He went down the beach and returned with a long, thin branch, some of our cord, and the ship's needle. He bent the needle into the shape of a hook, tied it to the cord, tied the cord to the branch, and ... "Hey presto, a fishing rod!" he said.

For bait, Peter used some of the oysters we'd found. He stood on the beach, casting his line into the shallows of the lagoon, and managed to catch a couple of fish straight away. But they were tiny, and Peter wasn't satisfied.

"This is no use ... " he muttered. "Big fish don't come into the shallows. I need to get out to the deeper water. I know – why don't we build a boat?"

"It would probably take far too long," said Jack, "if we could do it at all. And besides, I can't be bothered to wait – I'd like a nice big fish for dinner!"

We talked about building a raft, but realised it would take ages to chop down enough trees, and we had no rope to lash the logs together, anyway. In the end I suggested using just one tree, and that's what we agreed to do.

So we chopped down a tree growing near the water's edge. We trimmed off its branches, made three of them into rough paddles, and rolled the log into the sea. We had fun trying to sit on it, spending more time falling off to begin with. But we got the hang of it eventually, and soon we were out in the lagoon, me paddling at the front, Peter fishing from the middle, and Jack at the rear.

"I've got a bite!" Peter yelled almost immediately. He started pulling the fish in, and we could see through the clear water that it was a pretty big one.

I was as excited as Peter, but Jack's attention seemed to be elsewhere.

"Quick, let's get back to the beach," Jack hissed. "I can see … a shark!"

You can imagine the horror Peter and I felt when we heard this – our legs were dangling down into the water, and we were a long way from the shore. It was a big shark, and it came in fast, swimming round and round us, its sharp fin slicing through the calm water. We were far from calm. Peter had hauled his catch in, and we were paddling as fast as we could.

But the shark was getting closer and closer, almost playing with us. That terrifying black fin cut through the water like a knife through butter …

"Throw the fish to him, Peter!" Jack said in a loud whisper. "We might have a better chance of making it if he's distracted for a few moments … "

Peter followed Jack's orders, and no sooner had the fish fallen into the water than the shark rose, turned on its side to reveal a vast mouth full of razor-sharp teeth, and swallowed the fish whole. Then the deadly beast slid under the surface again, and came swimming towards us faster than ever.

"That was no good, boys," Jack muttered, his voice now tense and clipped. "So there's only one thing left to us. Now, do exactly as I tell you – our lives may depend on it. Keep paddling as fast as you can, don't look out for the shark, and don't glance behind you. Just make sure the log stays balanced!"

We did as Jack said, but I couldn't help glancing backwards. I saw Jack sitting very still, his paddle raised, the shark coming in close beneath the log, obviously just about to snap its jaws shut on Jack's foot. It was slowing down, almost as if it seemed sure of victory, a dark, evil shape in the blue water …

But Jack suddenly pulled his leg from the water, drew himself up as far as he could – and violently plunged his paddle right down the shark's throat. In fact, so violent was this act that the log rolled over, and all three of us were plunged into the lagoon. But we all rose instantly, spluttering and gasping. The shark was nowhere to be seen, although that didn't mean it had gone …

"Swim for shore!" yelled Jack, but Peter and I were already on our way.

A few moments later we dragged ourselves onto the white sands of the beach. We were safe, but we were exhausted, terrified by our ordeal.

SIX

Our encounter with the shark left the three of us feeling rather shaken. Up till then our stay on the island had almost seemed like a game, or at least an exciting adventure. It was true that we had faced great danger during the shipwreck, but we had survived, and made ourselves fairly comfortable.

But the sight of that fin slicing through the water had changed everything.

This was what my passion for roaming the wide world had brought me to, I thought – an existence where my life could be threatened every second of every day. And from what they said, I was sure Jack and Peter felt the same.

At any rate, that evening we sat round our fire and held a council of war. The time had come, as Jack said, to decide what we should do for the best. No ship had appeared, and we had no idea whether the captain had made it to another island. And we could wait a long time for someone else to find us.

"So we have a choice," said Jack at last. "We could build some sort of boat and try our luck on the seas … or we could explore the island, see if there is anyone here who could help us. What do you think, lads? Let's have a vote."

Peter and I looked at each other. Without saying a word, we both knew neither of us wanted to go to sea on a badly built raft or a leaky boat, and risk being caught in another storm – or worse, meeting that shark again.

"I vote for exploring the island," said Peter, and I nodded my agreement.

"Very well, that's settled then," said Jack, and we settled down for the night. Although I noticed that none of us mentioned the word cannibals …

I lay in the shelter, listening to the sound of surf booming on the reef. I thought of my mother and father, and wondered if I would ever see them, or whether I would end my days here in the South Seas I had so longed to visit.

I closed my eyes and thought about what tomorrow might bring.

Nicholas Nickleby

by Charles Dickens

Adapted by Steve Barlow and Steve Skidmore

THE STORY SO FAR *After the death of his father, nineteen-year-old Nicholas Nickleby is left penniless. Forced to earn a living, he becomes a teaching assistant at Dotheboys Hall, a school in Yorkshire, miles away from his family.*

Nicholas entered the schoolroom with Mr Squeers. He looked around with a heavy heart. The room was dark and dreary. The walls were dirty. Most of the glass in the windows was missing and the holes had been covered with old exercise books.

The brutish Head of Dotheboys Hall took up his position at the front of the class. In his dusty schoolmaster's jacket, and with his cane bent menacingly between his coarse hands, he made a forbidding spectacle. With his one eye, he gave the class of pale, silent boys a grim stare. Nicholas gazed in dismay at the poor, starved-looking creatures who stood in two lines, shivering with fear and cold.

Mrs Squeers stood at one of the rickety old desks. On it was a huge basin of brimstone and treacle.

"It's brimstone morning, Nickleby," explained Squeers. "We give it to the boys to purify their blood."

"Fiddlesticks!" sneered Mrs Squeers. "We give them brimstone and treacle because it spoils their appetites and is cheaper than breakfast and dinner."

As Nicholas watched in horror, Mrs Squeers began to dose the boys from a huge wooden spoon. All the boys took it in turn to be treacled, then staggered away holding their stomachs, and groaning.

"Now," said Squeers, giving the desk a great rap with his cane, which made half the little boys nearly jump out of their boots, "have you finished?"

"Yes," replied Mrs Squeers, choking the last boy in her hurry, and tapping the crown of his head with the wooden spoon to make him feel better. Then she took the empty basin and bustled out.

"Time for lessons!" said Squeers, beckoning Nicholas to stand beside him. "This is the first class in English spelling and practical learning, Nickleby. Now then, first boy! Smike, where is he?"

"Please, sir, he's cleaning the back-parlour window," said an older boy, trembling and cowering away from the headmaster.

"Ah, of course," said Squeers. "We follow the practical way of teaching, Nickleby. C-l-e-a-n, clean, verb active, to make bright. W-i-n, win, d-e-r, der, winder, a thing for looking out of. When the boy knows this out of the book, he goes and does it."

"I see," replied Nicholas, raising an eyebrow.

"Smike, where's the second boy?"

"Please, sir, he's weeding the garden," Smike replied in a faint voice.

"Good!" said Squeers. "B-o-t, bot, t-i-n, tin, bottin, n-e-y, bottinney, a knowledge of plants. When he has learned that bottinney means a knowledge of plants, he goes and knows 'em. That's our system, Nickleby: what do you think of it?"

"It's a very useful one," answered Nicholas.

Mr Squeers grinned. "The rest of the class, go and draw water from the pump. It's washing-day tomorrow, and we need the tubs filled."

So saying, Squeers dismissed the class to do their experiments in practical learning, and eyed Nicholas with a cunning look. "That's the way we do it, Nickleby."

Nicholas shrugged his shoulders. "So I see."

"And a very good way it is, too," said Squeers. "Now, just take them fourteen little boys and hear them some reading. You must begin to be useful and earn your keep. Idling about here won't do."

The children were arranged in a semi-circle round the new master, and he was soon listening to their dull, hesitant reading.

The morning dragged on. At one o'clock, the boys sat down in the kitchen to eat some hard salt beef. After this, there was another hour of crouching in the schoolroom and shivering with cold, and then 'lessons' began again.

The boys were assembled as Mr Squeers entered the room with a small bundle of letters in his hand. Mrs Squeers followed, carrying a pair of wicked-looking canes.

"Let any boy speak a word without leave," said Squeers, mildly, "and I'll take the skin off his back."

This announcement had the desired effect, and a death-like silence fell.

Mr Squeers cleared his throat and began.

"Boys, I've been to London, and have returned as strong and well as ever."

The boys gave three feeble cheers. Most wished that some misfortune could have fallen on the headmaster and so prevent his return.

"I have seen the parents of some boys," continued Squeers, "and they're so glad to hear how well their sons are getting on, that they want you to stay here as long as possible."

Mr Squeers ignored the snuffles from two or three of the boys at this news and continued. "I have had disappointments to contend with. Bolder's father was two pound ten short in his payment of fees. Come here, Bolder."

A wretched-looking boy stepped forward, quaking with fear.

"Bolder," said Squeers, moistening the palm of his right hand to get a good grip of the cane, "you're a young scoundrel, and as the last thrashing failed to beat the wickedness out of you, we must see what another will do."

With this, and ignoring Bolder's cry for mercy, Mr Squeers fell upon the boy and caned him soundly, not stopping until his arm was tired out.

"There," he said, when he had quite done. He turned to Smike and pointed. "Put him out, Smike."

Smike knew better, from long experience, than to hesitate about obeying. He bundled the victim out by a side door.

"Mobbs!" Another boy rose.

"Mobbs' step-mother," said Squeers, "has become ill on hearing that he refuses to eat fat and turns his nose up at cow's liver broth. She hopes Mr Squeers will flog him into a happier state of mind. Mobbs, come here!"

Mobbs moved slowly towards the desk, whereupon Mr Squeers carried out the invented wishes of Mobbs' step-mother.

Mr Squeers then proceeded to open some of the letters. Some of these enclosed money, which Mrs Squeers 'took care of'.

After this, there were a few slovenly lessons before Mr Squeers retired to his fireside. He left Nicholas to take care of the boys in the schoolroom.

There was a small stove in the corner nearest to the master's desk. Nicholas sat down by it. The cruelty he had witnessed, the behaviour of Mr Squeers, and the filth and misery he saw all around him made him feel helpless and depressed.

He was interrupted from his thoughts by Smike. The poor youth was on his knees before the stove, picking a few stray cinders from the hearth and planting them on the fire. He saw Nicholas looking at him and he shrunk back, as if expecting a blow.

"You need not fear me," said Nicholas, kindly. "Are you cold?"

"No," replied Smike, quickly. "I am used to it."

Smike was such a timid, broken-spirited creature, that Nicholas could not help exclaiming, "Poor fellow!"

Smike burst into tears. "Oh dear!" he cried, covering his face with his hands. "My heart will break. It will, it will."

"Hush!" said Nicholas, laying his hand upon his shoulder. "Be a man. How old are you?"

"Nineteen."

"And how long have you been here?"

"Since I was a little child. All those years of misery and beatings!" The tears coursed down Smike's face. "What misery I have suffered."

"There is always hope," said Nicholas – he didn't know what else to say.

"There is none for me," replied Smike. "Not like my friend Dorker."

"What of him?"

"He died," replied the youth. "I was with him that night. He said he saw faces round his bed that came from his home. He said they smiled, and talked to him. He died lifting his head up to kiss them … Are you still listening?"

"Yes," replied Nicholas.

"What faces will smile on me when I die?" cried Smike shivering. "Who will talk to me in those long nights? I have no home. I have no one! There is only pain and fear for me, alive or dead. I have no hope!"

The bell rang for bedtime and the boy crept away, leaving Nicholas with a heavy heart.

* * *

Over the following weeks, Mr Squeers came to regret employing Nicholas. The headmaster had thought an assistant would make him feel more important. This had not happened.

Mr Squeers had come to realise that Nicholas was kinder, more knowledgeable, and more of a gentleman than he could ever be. His hatred for Nicholas grew. Mr Squeers told himself that Nicholas was proud and stuck up. But he could not attack Nicholas openly, without admitting that he had made a mistake.

Smike had also changed. He now had a purpose to his life – to show his gratitude to Nicholas, the only person who had ever treated him like a human being. Realising that Nicholas cared for Smike, Mr Squeers took out his anger on the poor boy, and gave him beating after beating. Nicholas saw this, and ground his teeth at every savage and cowardly attack.

One night, Nicholas entered the schoolroom and saw Smike sitting in a corner. The poor soul was staring hard at a tattered book. He was trying to master some academic task, which any normal child of nine years old could have conquered with ease. However, for Smike, the exercise was a hopeless mystery.

"I can't do it," said Smike, looking up with bitter disappointment. He closed the book, laid his head upon his arm and began to weep.

"Do not cry," said Nicholas, "I cannot bear it."

"They have been beating me harder than ever," sobbed the boy.

"I know," replied Nicholas. "It is because of me. I am sorry."

"But for you," said Smike, "I should die. They would kill me; they would, I know they would."

Nicholas shook his head. "You will do better, poor fellow, when I am gone."

"Gone!" cried Smike, looking intently at him. "Are you leaving?"

"I cannot say," replied Nicholas. "I was speaking my own thoughts, out loud."

"Tell me," implored the boy, "will you go?"

"I shall be driven to it," said Nicholas. "I must leave and see the world."

"Is the world as bad and dismal as this place?"

"No," replied Nicholas. "Even its harshest moments do not compare to this."

At that moment, Mr Squeers entered and glared angrily at the boy. "Smike, you've got work to do!"

Smike sighed, put his book down, and followed the headmaster out of the room. Nicholas looked on helplessly.

* * *

It was a cold January morning and the feeble dawn light was stealing in at the cracked and grimy dormitory windows. Nicholas cast his eyes over the boys, shivering under their pitifully thin bundles of rags, looking for Smike. He couldn't find him.

The voice of Mr Squeers was heard, calling from the bottom of the stairs.

"Now then," cried that gentleman, "are you going to sleep all day, up there … "

" … you lazy hounds?" called up Mrs Squeers, finishing the sentence.

"We shall be down directly, sir," replied Nicholas.

"Down directly!" said Squeers. "Ah! You had better be down directly, or I'll be down upon some of you in less time than that. Where's that Smike?"

Nicholas looked hurriedly round again, but made no answer.

"Smike!" shouted Squeers.

"Do you want your head broke in a fresh place, Smike?" demanded Mrs Squeers.

Still there was no reply.

"Confound his impudence!" muttered Squeers, rapping the stair-rail impatiently with his cane. "Nickleby! Send that obstinate scoundrel down. Don't you hear me calling?"

"He is not here, sir," replied Nicholas.

"Don't tell me a lie," retorted the headmaster. "He is here."

"He is not here!" retorted Nicholas, angrily.

"We shall soon see about that," said Squeers, rushing upstairs. "I'll find him, I warrant you."

Mr Squeers burst into the dormitory, and darted into the corner where Smike usually slept.

There was nobody there.

"Where have you hid him?" said Squeers.

"I have seen nothing of him since last night," replied Nicholas.

"You won't save him this way. Where is he?"

"For all I know, at the bottom of the nearest pond," answered Nicholas.

Squeers turned on the other boys and began asking whether anyone knew where Smike was.

"Please, sir, I think Smike's run away, sir," piped up a voice.

"Ha!" cried Squeers. "Who said that?"

"Tomkins, sir," replied a chorus of voices.

Mr Squeers made a plunge into the crowd and grabbed hold of a small boy. "You think he has run away, do you, sir?" he demanded.

"Yes, please, sir," replied Tomkins.

Mr Squeers shook the frightened boy. "And what reason have you to suppose that any boy would want to run away from this establishment? Eh, sir?"

Mr Squeers didn't allow Tomkins to answer. Instead, he beat him.

"There," said Squeers. "Now if any other boy thinks Smike has run away, I shall be glad to have a talk with him."

There was a profound silence, during which Nicholas showed his disgust as plainly as he could.

"Well, Nickleby," said Squeers, eyeing him maliciously. "You think he has run away, I suppose?"

"I think it extremely likely," replied Nicholas, in a quiet manner.

"Oh, you do, do you?" sneered Squeers. "He didn't tell you he was going, I suppose, did he?"

"He did not," replied Nicholas. "I am very glad he did not. For then it would have been my duty to have warned you."

"Which you would not have wanted to, would you?" said Squeers, in a taunting fashion.

"No, I would not," replied Nicholas. "You interpret my feelings with great accuracy."

Mrs Squeers had listened to this conversation from the bottom of the stairs. But now, losing all patience, she made her way to the scene of action.

"What on earth are you a-talking to that Knuckleboy for, Squeers?"

"Why, my dear," said Squeers, "the fact is, that Smike is not to be found."

"Well, I know that," said the lady, "and where's the wonder? If you employ a proud teacher who makes the young dogs rebel, what do you expect?"

She turned to Nicholas. "Now, young man, take yourself and the boys off to the schoolroom, and don't you leave until I give you permission." She glared at Nicholas. "I wouldn't keep you in the house a minute longer, if I had my way."

"And I wouldn't be here if I had mine," replied Nicholas. "Now, boys!"

"Ah! Now, boys," said Mrs Squeers, mimicking Nicholas. "Follow your leader! And follow Smike if you dare. You'll see what I'll do to him, when I get back. And if any of you mention his name, he'll have it twice as bad."

"If he has run away and I catch him," said Squeers, "I'll only stop short of flaying him alive."

Mrs Squeers gave a snort of disgust. "Of course he's run away."

"How can you be so sure?" asked Squeers.

"He's not downstairs, and the cow-house and stable are locked up, so he can't be there. He must have gone to York along the public road."

"Why must he?" inquired Squeers.

"Stupid!" said Mrs Squeers, angrily. "He hasn't got any money, has he?"

"He's never had a penny in his whole life."

"Then he must beg his way, and he could only do that on the public road," said Mrs Squeers.

"That's true!" exclaimed Squeers, clapping his hands.

"True! Yes, but you would never have thought of it, if I hadn't said so," replied his wife. "Now, if you take the cart and go down one road, I'll borrow another cart and go the other. If we ask questions and keep our eyes open, one of us is certain to find him."

"And when we do … " Squeers swished his cane furiously in the air as Nicholas looked on, eyeing the pair with pure hatred.

Mrs Squeers' plan was adopted and put into execution. After a hasty breakfast, Mr Squeers set off, intent upon vengeance. Shortly afterwards, Mrs Squeers drove out in another cart and in a different direction. She took with her a wooden cudgel and several pieces of strong cord.

Nicholas remained behind, wondering what would happen to Smike. Death, from hunger and exposure to the weather, was the best that could be expected for so poor and helpless a creature. There was little to choose between this fate and a return to the school.

He was in this state of anxiety until the evening of the next day, when Mr Squeers returned, alone, and unsuccessful.

"No news of the scamp!" said the headmaster. He gave Nicholas a hard look. "Someone will pay for this, Nickleby, if Mrs Squeers don't hunt him down. Mark my words."

The sound of a cart from outside, followed by cries of pain and fear, interrupted them.

Mrs Squeers entered, followed by the wretched Smike. He was covered in mud and rain, and looked haggard. His arms were tied together. Trembling with delight, Mr Squeers unloosened the cord.

The rest of the boys were called down to witness Smike's punishment. Mr Squeers and his wife stood glaring at the assembled throng.

Smike shook with terror.

"Each boy keep his place," said Squeers. "Nickleby! To your desk, sir."

Tight-lipped, Nicholas obeyed.

"Have you anything to say, Smike?" demanded Squeers, swishing his cane in the air.

"Spare me, sir!" cried Smike.

"Oh, that's all, is it?" said Squeers. "Yes, I'll flog you within an inch of your life, and spare you that."

"Ha, ha, ha!" laughed Mrs Squeers. "That's a good 'un!"

"I was driven to do it," said Smike, faintly.

"Driven to do it, were you?" said Squeers. "Oh, it wasn't your fault; it was mine, I suppose – eh?"

"You're a nasty, ungrateful, pig-headed, brutish, obstinate, sneaking dog," exclaimed Mrs Squeers, taking Smike's head under her arm. "What do you mean, you were driven to do it?"

"Stand aside, my dear," replied Squeers. "We'll try and find out." He held Smike firmly in his grip, and hit him with his cane. Ignoring the boy's scream of pain, the headmaster raised his cane again.

"Stop!" cried Nicholas, in a voice that made the rafters ring.

"Who cried 'stop'?" demanded Squeers, turning round savagely.

"I," said Nicholas, stepping forward. "This must not go on."

"Must not go on?" shrieked Squeers.

"No!" thundered Nicholas.

Stunned by the boldness of Nicholas' interference, Mr Squeers released his hold on Smike, and gazed upon Nicholas with looks that were positively frightful.

"Must not, I say," repeated Nicholas. "*Shall* not. I will prevent it."

Mr Squeers continued to gaze upon him with bulging eyes.

"Do not blame me for this public interference," said Nicholas. "You have brought it upon yourself."

"Sit down, beggar!" screamed Squeers, almost beside himself with rage. He grabbed hold of Smike as he spoke.

"Wretch!" warned Nicholas, fiercely. "Touch him at your peril! I will not stand by, and see it done. My blood is up, and I have the strength of ten men."

"Stand back," cried Squeers, brandishing his cane.

"You have insulted me many times," said Nicholas, flushed with passion. "Your cruelty towards these boys has been terrible! Have a care –

for if you do not stop, I will not spare you!"

He had scarcely spoken, when Mr Squeers,
with a cry like the howl of a wild beast, struck
him a blow across the face.

Smarting with the agony of the blow, Nicholas
sprang upon Mr Squeers. He snatched the
weapon from the headmaster's hand, and beat the
brute until he roared for mercy.

Mrs Squeers rushed to her husband's defence.

She grabbed hold of her partner's coat, and tried to drag him free. Failing to do this, she turned on Nicholas and began to beat him to her heart's content.

Nicholas hardly felt the blows. He flung Mr Squeers away from him with all the force he could muster. Mr Squeers fell back against his wife and both crashed downwards. The headmaster's head struck the stone floor and he lay on the ground, stunned.

The fight was over. Nicholas looked around at the happy faces of the schoolboys.

Smike dropped to knees. "Sir, Mr Nickleby. May I leave with you?" he begged. "I cannot stay here with these people. I will be your faithful hard-working servant."

Nicholas smiled. "So you shall. We will leave this terrible place together."

The boys cheered as Nicholas and Smike stepped over the groaning bodies of Mr and Mrs Squeers. With a final wave, Nicholas and Smike left Dotheboys Hall and walked off to face whatever the world had in store for them.

THE PIT AND THE PENDULUM

By Edgar Allan Poe
Adapted by Geoff Reilly

The story is set in Spain, in the prison in Toledo. It is about 1500. The narrator has been tortured by a mysterious and powerful religious organisation, known as the Spanish Inquisition. Tried in court for crimes that are not revealed to the reader, he is finally sentenced to death. He collapses and faints.

So far, I had not opened my eyes. I felt that I lay upon my back, so I reached out my hand, and it fell heavily upon something damp and hard. I let it lie there for many minutes, while I struggled to imagine where I could be. At last, with a wild desperation, I quickly opened my eyes, dreading what I might see.

I lay in total blackness. Terrified, I struggled for breath. The intensity of the darkness seemed to weigh me down. I made myself lie quietly and think. I had been sentenced to death and it appeared to me that a very long time had passed since that moment. Yet, I was not dead.

Usually, the condemned were executed the same day. Had I been returned to my cell, to await execution? This could not be, because all the condemned cells at Toledo had stone floors, and allowed some light in, even at night. Yet, I remained in total blackness.

As I got to my feet, I was trembling convulsively. I thrust my arms wildly around me in all directions. I felt nothing; yet I dreaded to move a step, in case I was in a TOMB. Sweat burst from every pore, and stood in cold, big beads upon my forehead. The agony of suspense grew unbearable, and so I cautiously moved forward, with my arms extended, and my eyes straining from their sockets, in the hope of catching some faint ray of light. I staggered for many paces, with hands outstretched, meeting nothing but dark emptiness.

My mind was filled with imaginings and the thousand vague rumours that I remembered of the horrors of Toledo prison. Strange stories were whispered about the dungeons of Toledo. They all ended in death. That was certain.

My outstretched hands finally met something solid. It was a stone wall – very smooth, slimy, and cold. I needed to find out how big my prison was. I decided that I needed a way of marking my starting point, then I could feel my way around the walls until I returned to my marker.

The only thing I had was the rough clothing that I wore. Tearing a strip from my tunic, I placed it on the floor, where I could not miss it when I returned. However, I had not realised the size of the dungeon, or my own weakness. The ground was moist and slippery. I staggered onward for some time, until I stumbled and fell. My exhaustion left me lying on the floor, and sleep overcame me.

When I awoke, and stretched out my arm, I found a loaf of bread and a jug of water beside me. I was too exhausted to wonder where they had come from, but ate and drank greedily. Shortly afterwards, I managed to make a journey

around my prison. I guessed the circuit of the cell to be about fifty metres. However, there were so many angles in the walls that I could not guess its shape.

Gathering confidence from my successful journey around the walls, I decided to explore the centre of the cell. At first, I moved with extreme caution, for the floor was treacherous with slime. Finally, I gathered my courage and walked boldly into the centre.

I had walked some ten or twelve paces in this way, when the torn hem of my robe became entangled between my legs. I stepped on it, and fell violently on my face.

Dazed, I did not realise my position for a few moments. My chin was resting on the floor of the cell, but my lips, and the upper part of my head, touched nothing. At the same time, my forehead seemed bathed in a clammy vapour, and the peculiar smell of decayed fungus rose to my nostrils. I reached out and shuddered to find that I had fallen at the very edge of a circular pit.

Groping around the stonework just below the edge of the pit, I succeeded in dislodging a small stone, and dropped it into the abyss. For many seconds I listened to the sound of it bouncing off the walls of the chasm as it fell. Finally, the stone met water and the echoes faded slowly in the dark. At the same time there came a sound like the quick opening, and rapid closing, of a door overhead, and a faint gleam of light flashed suddenly through the gloom; then, just as suddenly, it faded away.

I saw clearly that if I had taken another step, I would have fallen to my death.

Shaking in every limb, I groped my way back to the wall – deciding to die there rather than risk the horrors of the pit. Mentally exhausted, I fell asleep again. Upon waking, I found by my side, as before, a loaf of bread and a jug of water. I was so thirsty that I emptied the jug in one go. It must have been drugged, for I became sleepy  and I fell into a deep sleep – a sleep like death. How long it lasted, I do not know; but when I opened my eyes, I found that there was a dim, yellow light. I lay for some time pondering my situation and gazing around my prison cell.

I found that I had been wrong about the size of the cell. It could not have been more than twenty-five paces around the walls. I had been deceived, too, about the shape of the room. The general shape of the cell was square. What I had taken for stonework seemed now to be iron, or some other metal, in huge plates. The entire surface of this metal cell was crudely painted with the figures of devils, skeletons and other more fearful images.

I found that I could not see many details because, while I had been unconscious, I had been securely tied to a low framework of wood. This left only my head and the lower part of my left arm free, so that I could reach some food from a clay dish which lay by my side on the floor. The food in the dish was a strong-smelling, greasy meat. Then, I saw to my horror that the jug had been removed. I say to my horror, for I was unbearably thirsty. It was clear that my torturers wanted me to suffer from thirst!

Looking up, I examined the ceiling of my cell. It was some ten or twelve metres high, and was made of metal in the same way as the walls. On one of its panels was the painted figure of Time. He was painted as an old man with a white beard and flowing hair. He seemed to gaze directly down at me. Yet, unlike most pictures of Time, instead of a scythe, he seemed to be holding a huge pendulum, such as we see on antique clocks. There was something, however, in the appearance of this pendulum, which caused me to watch it more closely. While I gazed directly upward at it, I imagined that it was moving. Seconds later, I discovered I was right. Its movement was slow. I watched it for some minutes, in fear and wonder. Eventually, tired of watching it, I turned my head to look around the cell.

A slight noise attracted my attention, and looking at the floor, I saw several enormous rats scurrying across it. They had crept out of the pit, which I could just see. Even as I watched, more rats rose over the edge, with ravenous eyes, drawn by the scent of meat.

It might have been half-an-hour, perhaps even an hour, before I looked upwards again. What I saw horrified me. The sweep of the pendulum had increased by nearly a metre. It had also increased in the speed of its movement. But what really terrified me was that it was getting lower. As I gazed in terror at the pendulum, I saw that it was made in the shape of a crescent of glittering steel, about a metre in length, and the lower edge was obviously as sharp as a razor. It was attached to a heavy rod of brass, and the whole thing HISSED as it swung through the air.

I lay for long, long hours of horror, during which I counted the rushing movements of the steel pendulum! Inch by inch – line by line – down and down it came! Long, long hours passed before it swept so closely over me that I could feel the rush of air as it passed. The smell of the sharp steel forced itself into my nostrils. All I wanted was for it to be over. I prayed and I wept. I grew frantic and a little mad, trying to end it all by forcing myself upward into the sweep of the terrifying blade. Anything, just to end the torture!

At last, I became oddly calm, and lay smiling insanely at the glittering blade. I blacked out once more. When I recovered, I felt sick and weak. I was by now half-mad.

The swing of the pendulum was at right angles to my body, designed to cross my heart. I realised that it would slowly cut the threads of my robe. It would return and repeat its actions – to the right – to the left – far and wide. Despite its wide sweep (some ten metres or more) and the hissing speed of its descent, it would only cut a few threads for quite some time, before it began to slice into me. I found myself concentrating on the sound of the blade as it passed across the robe.

Down – steadily it crept down.

Down – relentlessly down! It vibrated within three inches of my chest! I struggled violently – furiously – to free my left arm completely.

Down – still the pendulum came down!

I gasped and struggled at each hissing pass. I shrunk away from it at every sweep of the blade. My eyes followed its upward sweep, though they closed themselves tightly as it came down. It looked as if ten or twelve huge swings would bring the steel into contact with my robe, and I began to despair.

It suddenly occurred to me that I was tied to my framework by a single rope that had been wound round and round my body and limbs.

The first stroke of the razor-like blade across any part of the rope would loosen the rest because of the way that my torturers had tied it. If just one part of the rope that was wound around me became loose, I could use my left hand to untie my bonds. But if I raised myself at the wrong moment, or just a fraction too high, I would meet the blade all the sooner!

Judging the moment carefully, I raised my head to examine the position of the rope. In frustration, I cried out when I saw that the rope bound me everywhere, except in the path of the pendulum. As things stood, the blade would not cut the rope.

I dropped my head back. I lay in despair for many minutes, before another desperate plan formed in my mind. For many hours, the area around my low framework had been swarming with rats. They were wild, bold, ravenous, their red eyes glaring at me as if they waited only for me to be still, to make me their prey.

They had devoured everything except a small part of the contents of my dish, despite my feeble waving of my hand, in an effort to keep them away from my scraps of food. With the remains of the oily food, I carefully rubbed the rope wherever I could reach it; then I lay breathlessly still.

At first, the rats were cautious. Seeing no movement from me, one or two of the boldest leaped up on the framework and sniffed at the rope. More rats climbed out of the pit.

They climbed onto my framework in their hundreds and scurried over me. The movement of the pendulum did not disturb them at all. Avoiding its swings, they gnawed the tasty rope. They swarmed over me in growing numbers. They scuttled over my throat; their cold noses touched my lips. I was disgusted and horrified, yet I could see a loosening of the rope. I knew that in more than one place it had already been chewed through.

With determination, waiting for the next swing of the pendulum, I forced myself to lie still. At last, I felt the rope sag and realised that I would soon be FREE. But the stroke of the pendulum had already touched my chest. It had cut the material of the robe. Twice again it swung, and a sharp pain shot through every nerve, as it parted the skin on my chest. But the moment of escape had arrived. At the movement of my hand, the rats scurried away, shrieking. With a careful movement, I slid from the embrace of the rope and beyond the reach of the pendulum. For the moment, at least, I WAS FREE.

I had hardly stepped from my wooden bed of horror onto the stone floor of the prison, when the movement of the pendulum stopped, and it silently disappeared into an opening in the ceiling. I then realised that I was being watched, all the time. So what horror would they inflict on me now? I glanced nervously around the iron walls.

Some unusual change had taken place in the walls. I became aware, for the first time, of the origin of the light which illuminated the cell. It came from a gap about half-an-inch wide at the base of the walls. I tried to look through the gap, without success.

Suddenly I realised that the outlines of the painted figures on the walls had now become startlingly and intensely bright. There came to my nostrils the smell of heated iron! A suffocating smell crawled through my prison. A richer shade of crimson spread over the painted walls. I panted, I gasped for breath! I shrank away from the glowing metal walls towards the centre of the cell. As the heat increased, the thought of the coolness of the pit attracted me to its edge.

The heat now rapidly increased, and I looked up, shuddering as if I had a fever. There had been a second change in the cell. The room had been square. Now the walls were moving with a low rumbling or moaning sound! My torturers wanted the burning iron walls to force me INTO THE PIT. With a scream, I leaped away from the edge and buried my face in my hands – weeping bitterly. I cowered, but the creeping walls pushed me back towards the edge of the pit. Finally, there was no room for my scorched and battered body on the firm floor of the prison. With one loud, long, and final scream of despair, I averted my eyes, staggering on the very edge of the pit.

Suddenly, there was the loud and urgent sound of human voices! There was a harsh grating sound, like a thousand thunders! The fiery walls drew back! A strong hand caught my arm as I fell, fainting, backwards into the pit.